Adios, Coyote

Marcia Vaughan

Illustrated by Mini Goss

Rigby

Contents

CHAPTER 1

Oh, Coyote

Oh, Coyote. That pesky prankster had a bad habit of playing low-down, dirty tricks on the other desert animals.

"Coyote invited me to dinner, then tried to put me in the frying pan," Quail complained to his friends one morning.

Road Runner said, "Coyote challenged me to a race, but the race ended in a trap. And I lost my tail feathers trying to escape."

"If you think that's bad," Prairie Dog added. "Coyote painted the rock outside my burrow to look like a bobcat. I was so scared I didn't come out for a week."

CHAPTER 2
A Secret Meeting

In time, Coyote's tricks became so troublesome that one star-bright night, Jackrabbit called a secret meeting under the Joshua tree.

"Reckon it's time Coyote had a taste of trouble himself," Jackrabbit said to the others.

"What can we do?" asked Wild
Pig Javelina. "Coyote is cunning
and clever and cruel."

Jackrabbit stamped his foot. "We've got to trick him once, twice, three times. Then that bothersome bully will be done for good."

"How?" asked the others.

As the moon rolled across the desert sky, Jackrabbit whispered his secret plan.

CHAPTER 3

The Giant Hairy Scorpion Trick

The next day, Coyote woke up and scratched his flea-bitten belly. "Hi-de-hay, who will I trick today?" he wondered. "How about that Giant Hairy Scorpion."

Coyote tramped through the tumbleweeds. He found Scorpion down by the creek. Scorpion was rubbing sagebush back and forth over something brown and round.

"Hey, Giant Hairy Scorpion," Coyote called. "What are you doing with that sagebush?"

"What does it look like I'm doing?" Scorpion replied. "I'm dusting off this big hunk of trouble."

Coyote blinked his eyes.

"Doesn't look like trouble to me," he said. "That there looks more like an old, dry mud pie."

"Coyote, you must be blind as a bat," Scorpion snapped. "This is not a mud pie. No siree, this is Big Bobcat's new flat hat. I'm supposed to dust it off so he can wear it to meet his girlfriend."

Coyote snickered. "And who would Big Bobcat's girlfriend be?"

"Why, it's Miss Armadillo, of course."

Coyote's eyes opened wide.

"Miss Armadillo is MY girl-friend!" he growled, swishing his tail from side to side.

"Not after she sees Big Bobcat wearing this handsome new hat," Scorpion said.

"Cooeee," cried Coyote. "Give me that hat, quick."

"Can't," said Scorpion. "Big Bobcat told me to make sure and certain nobody touches it, or there'll be trouble. Big trouble."

"Looky here, you squishy little bug," Coyote said. "Either I wear that hat on my head or I wear you!"

"All right," Scorpion shrugged.

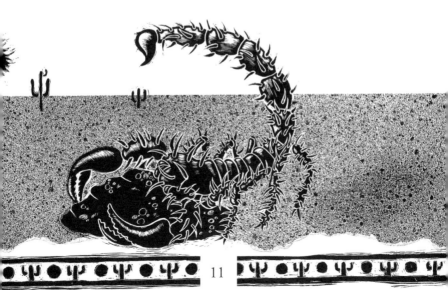

Off behind the river rocks Scorpion scampered, singing softly, "Don't mess with trouble, whatever you do. 'Cause if you mess with trouble, it will mess with you."

Coyote snatched up the mud pie and set it carefully on top of his

head. Then *boomba, boomba, boomba*, Miss Armadillo came strutting along, her shell shining like silver in the sunlight.

Coyote bowed low. "Morning, Miss Armadillo. Reckon I'd be happy as a fly stuck in honey if you'd take a walk with me today. I wore this fine, flat hat so you'd know just what I think of you."

Miss Armadillo took one look at that round, brown mud pie all covered with flies, and leaped into the air shrieking.

"You disgusting old coyote. I never want to see you again!" she snapped.

Down the trail she stomped— *boomba, boomba, boom.*

"I told you not to mess with trouble," called Scorpion. "But you didn't listen. No siree."

CHAPTER 4

The Pig-Headed Javelina Trick

The next day, Coyote woke up and scratched his flea-bitten belly. "Hi-de-hay, who will I trick today?" he wondered. "How about that pig-headed Javelina."

Coyote found Javelina down at the purple prickly pear patch. That wild pig was tiptoeing in circles around a sleeping animal.

"Javelina," Coyote called. "What have you got there?"

"Trouble," whispered Javelina, going around and around.

Coyote blinked his eyes. "Doesn't look like trouble to me," he said. "That there looks more like a furry little lump."

"Coyote, you must have dust for brains," snorted Javelina. "This

lump is Big Bobcat's new pet cat. See here, it's got a fancy white stripe running all the way down its fine black back. I'm supposed to take care of it, so you best mosey along."

"Cooeee," said Coyote. "Never, in my live-long life, have I patted a white-striped cat. I'll bet Big Bobcat won't mind if I give it just one pint-sized pat."

"He will, too," Javelina argued. "Big Bobcat told me to make sure and certain nobody pats his cat, or there'll be trouble. Big trouble."

"Looky here, you hairy hog," Coyote snapped. "Either I pat this white-striped cat or I pat YOU till you're flat."

"All right," Javelina sighed.

Off behind the cactus trotted Javelina, singing, "Don't mess with trouble, whatever you do. 'Cause if you mess with trouble, it will mess with you."

With a big ol' grin, Coyote bent over and patted that skunk from the top of her head to the tip of her tail.

That pat riled the skunk up
something fierce. She raised her
white-striped tail in the air and
sprayed Coyote a good one.

"Yuckeroo!" Coyote howled, leaping in the air. He landed with a thud in the mud in the middle of the nearest waterhole. He scrubbed his stinky self—nose to toes.

"I told you not to mess with trouble," snorted Javelina. "But you didn't listen. Huh, uh."

CHAPTER 5
The Jumpy Jackrabbit Trick

The next day, Coyote woke up and scratched his flea-bitten belly. "Hi-de-hay, who will I trick today?" he wondered. "How about that jumpy Jackrabbit."

Coyote found Jackrabbit down by a stand of cottonwood trees. It looked to Coyote like Jackrabbit was hip-hopping back and forth under the tallest tree.

"Jackrabbit," Coyote called. "Why are you hopping?"

"Got to," replied Jackrabbit, wiping his brow. "I'm guarding the trouble that hangs in this tree."

Coyote blinked. "Doesn't look like trouble to me," he said, staring at the branch. "That there looks more like a dusty old drum."

"Coyote, I reckon you're just about as smart as a stump," Jackrabbit said. "That's not just any dusty old drum. It's Big Bobcat's wishing drum. He plays it any time he wants a wish to come true."

"Cooeee," said Coyote. "In all my howling, prowling days I've never played a wishing drum. Big Bobcat will never know if I bang it just once."

Jackrabbit shook his head. "Can't let you. Big Bobcat told me to make sure and certain nobody plays his drum, or there'll be trouble. Big trouble."

Coyote snarled and snapped his teeth. "Looky here, you hare-brained hopper," he growled, "either I bang on this drum, or I bang on YOU!"

"All right," said Jackrabbit.

Off behind the cottonwoods dashed Jackrabbit, singing, "Don't

mess with trouble, whatever you do.
'Cause if you mess with trouble, it
will mess with you!"

Coyote closed his eyes and
thought hard. "I wish with all my
whiskers never to see that squishy
scorpion, that prickly pig, or that
hare-brained hopper ever again."

Then he picked up a stick and
BAP, BAP, BAP! Coyote whacked
that hornet's nest as hard as he
could.

Ooo-eee. Those hornets didn't
take kindly to that sort of howdy-
do. No siree. They came storming
out of that nest like a twirling
tornado.

"Yow-ow-ow-ow-ow!" howled Coyote, as hundreds of hornets stung him up one side and down the other.

That angry swarm chased Coyote in and out of the cottonwoods, all around the prickly pear patch, through the river, across the desert, and clean out of sight.

"Adios, Coyote," Jackrabbit hollered after him. "Looks like that drum made your wish and OUR wish come true.

"Don't mess with trouble, whatever you do. 'Cause if you mess with trouble, it will mess with you!"